THE CYBIL WAR

ALSO BY BETSY BYARS

After the Goat Man
The Cartoonist
The Eighteenth Emergency
Good-bye, Chicken Little
The House of Wings
The Night Swimmers
The Pinballs
The TV Kid
The Winged Colt of Casa Mia

THE
CYBIL WAR
Betsy Byars

THE BODLEY HEAD
LONDON SYDNEY
TORONTO

British Library Cataloguing
in Publication Data
Byars, Betsy
The Cybil war.
I. Title
823'.9'1F
ISBN 0-370-30426-8

Copyright © 1981 by Betsy Byars
All rights reserved
Printed in Great Britain for
The Bodley Head Ltd
9 Bow Street, London WC2E 7AL
by Redwood Burn Ltd,
Trowbridge & Esher
Phototypeset in Linotron 202 Baskerville
by Western Printing Services Ltd, Bristol
*First published by Viking Press, Inc.,
New York, 1981*
First published in Great Britain 1981

Being Ms Indigestion

Simon was at his desk, slumped, staring at the dull wood. Someone had once carved "I hate school" in the wood, and over the years others had worked on the letters so that now they were as deep as a motto in stone.

Simon sighed. His teacher, clipboard in hand, was choosing the cast of a nutrition play. She had already cast Tony Angotti as the dill pickle which meant that he, another of her non-favourites, would probably be the Swiss cheese. The thought of himself in a yellow box full of holes made him miserable. He had never been one for costumes—even at Hallowe'en he limited himself to a mask—and now this. Well, he would just have to be absent that day.

Miss McFawn cast Laura Goode and Melissa Holbrook as the green beans.

"Good casting," Tony Angotti said. "You guys look like green beans when you turn sideways."

Simon smiled.

"Frontways you look like spaghetti."

Simon laughed, and Laura Goode hit him on the arm with her music book.

"I didn't say it," Simon protested.

"You laughed."

He turned away. "Violence is not characteristic of the green bean," he said coldly. His arm hurt but he refused to rub it.

He waited, without hope, while Miss McFawn cast Billy Bonfili as the hot dog, Wanda Sanchez as the bun. Slowly he realized that the entire play had been cast. Bananas, tacos, onions, pecans surrounded him. He alone had no role.

"Let's see," Miss McFawn said, "who can we get to be Mr Indigestion?"

Mr Indigestion! Simon couldn't believe it. This was the lead role. She could only be doing it out of spite, he knew that, but still he really wanted to be Mr Indigestion. He who had walked along in misery last Hallowe'en in his Jimmy Carter mask while Tony Angotti romped beside him in his mother's dress stuffed with balloons, *he* now actually wanted to put on a black cape and moustache and twirl on stage as Mr Indigestion. He was surprised at himself.

"Oh, yes," she said. "Simon can be Mr Indigestion." She made a note on her clipboard. "Simon will be the perfect indigestion."

"It takes one to know one," Tony Angotti muttered.

Everyone around Tony snickered and Miss McFawn looked at him. Miss McFawn could stare down a cobra. In three seconds Tony's eyes were on his desk.

In the pause that followed, Cybil Ackerman called

6

from the back of the room. "Miss McFawn?"

Miss McFawn's eyes were still on Tony Angotti in case he was fool enough to look up again. He was not and Miss McFawn's eyes shifted to Cybil.

"Miss McFawn?"

"Yes, Cybil, what is it?"

"Well, every time we have a play the boys get all the good parts. When we did the ecology play, the girls had to be trees and flowers while the boys got to be forest fires and coal mines and nuclear waste. And when we did the geography parade, the boys got to be countries like Russia and China, and we had to be Holland and the Virgin Islands. It's not fair."

"What do you suggest, Cybil?"

"I think we ought to have a *Ms* Indigestion."

Simon swirled round in his seat. He felt as cheated as a dog deprived of a sirloin steak. His mouth was open. He tried to give her a McFawn stare-down, but she was looking over his head.

"We could vote on it," she said nicely.

"That's not fair," Simon said. There were seventeen girls in the room and fourteen boys. He turned back to Miss McFawn. "All the girls will vote for Ms Indigestion."

"We will not!" the girls said in chorus. They were used to voting in a bloc.

"All right, that's a good idea. We'll vote," Miss McFawn said. Simon thought she looked at him with satisfaction. "How many would like to have a Ms Indigestion?"

Seventeen girls raised their hands.

"How many for Mr Indigestion?"

Fourteen boys raised their hands. Tony Angotti had two hands up, one positioned to appear to be Wanda Sanchez's, but Miss McFawn was not fooled.

"Ms Indigestion it is," Miss McFawn said in a pleased voice. She crossed out Simon's name on her list. "Let's see. Cybil, would you like to be Ms Indigestion?"

"Yes!"

"So what's Simon going to be?" Tony Angotti asked. He was not going to be the dill pickle unless everybody else was something.

"He can have my part," Cybil offered.

"Or mine," Tony said. "I have the feeling I'm going to be absent that day."

"No, Tony, I especially want you to be the dill pickle." Miss McFawn checked her list of players and foods. "Let's see, we could do with another starch. All right, Simon, you can either be a macaroni and cheese pie or—what were you, Cybil?"

"A jar of peanut butter."

"Or be a jar of peanut butter."

Simon kept his eyes on his desk. He stared at the phrase "I hate school" so hard that he expected the words to catch fire.

"I'll have to have your decision, Simon."

He did not move. He felt betrayed. For the first time in his life, he had actually been willing to put on a costume, come out on stage, twirling his moustache, even saying, "I am the dreadful Mr Indigestion," only to have it taken away.

"Simon," she prompted.

He mumbled something without taking his eyes from the letters on his desk. Now he was actually willing them to catch fire, like Superman.

"I'm sorry, Simon, I didn't hear you. You'll have to speak up. What do you want to be?"

"A jar of peanut butter!"

"Violence is not characteristic of peanut butter," Laura Goode sneered.

Simon struck at her, hitting his hand on the back of her desk. Pain shot all the way up to his shoulder.

"Miss McFawn, Simon hit me," Laura called happily.

"Simon, I'm not going to have violence in my classroom."

Simon looked up at Miss McFawn. He stared at her with the same intensity and hatred he had stared at the letters on his desk.

For the first time that anyone could remember, it was Miss McFawn who looked away.

"Rehearsal Friday," she reminded them as she shifted the papers on her desk.

Arbor Day is for the Birds

Simon, eyes on his book, felt his face burn. He had made a fool of himself, and over nothing. Over being Mr Indigestion, which nobody in their right mind would want to be.

"Tony, will you explain what the poet means?" Miss McFawn was asking.

"He means," Tony said slowly, stalling for time, "he *means*, now, wait a minute . . ."

"Wanda?"

"He means that things are not what they seem."

"Very good!"

And what really hurt, Simon told himself—he was sitting with his eyes on the wrong page, finger marking the wrong poem—what really hurt was that Cybil Ackerman had a part in his humiliation. And he was in love with Cybil Ackerman, had been for three years.

He had fallen in love with her in the room right below this one. It was Arbor Day, and their teacher Miss Ellis made a big thing out of it. She gave every student a little tree to take home and plant, and the celebration was capped off with the writing and reading of tributes to trees.

Simon had been careful with his baby tree. Some of the other boys were using theirs in whip battles and trying to see how high they could throw them. Not Simon. He was taking his home in the crook of his arm, like a real baby, so his father could help him plant it. It was the first time he had something he was sure his father would want to do.

He went into the house, and his mother was standing in the kitchen. He said, "Look, I've got this baby tree and Dad and I are going to plant it and watch it grow and . . ."

"Your dad cannot help you plant that tree," his mother said tiredly. "Your dad's gone."

"Well, I'll wait till he gets back. I'll put the tree in a little bucket. I'll water it. I'll . . ."

"Simon, look at me." She sat down on a chair so that their heads were level. "Now, your dad's gone. We've been over this and over this. No, don't turn away. Your dad is gone and I do not know where he is or when he's coming back. Do you understand me?"

He tried to look away, but she held his head in place with her hand. He blinked uneasily. He was aware his mother had been talking to him about his father's absence, probably for days, but for the first time he realized what she was talking about.

"When will he be back?"

"I don't know."

"Well, where has he gone?"

"All I know is this. He has gone. His clothes are gone. The car is gone. The camping equipment is gone. Half the money in our bank account is gone."

"It's business . . . it's vacation . . . " he stuttered.

"No, he's gone."

It was more than he could stand—that his father, the only person he could not live without, could actually decide to live without him. The earth seemed to tremble with a terrible inner quake.

"Maybe he's dead," he said, his voice reflecting the quivering world.

"He's not dead."

"How do you know? He could be. People die. Their bodies are never found."

"It turns out he's been talking to Mitch Wilson about leaving for months."

"What did he say?"

"Oh, he talked about solitude and about getting away from the confusion and corruption of the world and going back to the simple way of life and about living off the land and about . . ."

"It has to be more than that. It has to be!"

Suddenly Simon turned, pulling away from his mother. He looked down. He was clutching the baby tree in both hands as if he were trying to choke it. He ran from the room.

"Simon, he'll be back some time. I know he will," his mother called. "It's just something he's going through and we'll get along." She followed him to the back door. "Simon, I can't give you answers because he didn't give them to me!"

Simon ran into the backyard and threw his baby

tree as far as he could. He didn't see it land because his hands were over his eyes, but in his mind that baby tree went so high and so far nobody ever saw it again.

When it came to the reading of tributes to trees, Simon was the first to volunteer. He read in a loud, hard voice:

> I hate Arbor Day. I hate trees.
> I'm going to chop down every tree I see.

He had to lean close to read his writing. He had pressed down so hard with his pencil that he'd gone through the paper in three places.

There was a gasp from Miss Ellis. "That is enough!" She made her way to the front of the room in three steps. She took the paper from him so violently that she tore off the corner. Then she ripped the rest into pieces and threw them into the trash can.

"Sit, Simon," she said.

He had heard kinder tones used on dogs. He walked back to his desk with his head held so high he stumbled over Billy Bonfili's foot.

In a voice still trembling with rage, Miss Ellis called on Wanda Sanchez. Wanda made a lot of noise walking to the front of the room because she, too, was outraged about Simon's tribute to trees.

Her composition went:

The tree is a gift from God. It
gives us shade. It gives us wood. It
gives us food. Thank you, God, for trees.

"Thank *you*, Wanda," Miss Ellis said.

"You're *welcome*, Miss Ellis."

When all the children had read their tributes, Miss
Ellis announced that they would have a vote on
whose paper was the best. Wanda Sanchez, the
favourite, got nine votes. Tony Angotti got five. He
had written a comic tribute to trees, pointing out that
if there were no trees, birds would have to build nests
on top of people's heads.

"Oh, Miss Ellis," Cybil Ackerman called from the
back of the room when the voting was over.

"Yes, Cybil?"

"You forgot to call Simon's name."

There was a pause while Miss Ellis inhaled and
exhaled. "I don't think anyone wants to vote for
Simon's paper," she said, "do they?"

She sounded as if she was asking if anyone wanted
to vote for a fungus infection.

Simon put his hand up so high his arm hurt.

There was another icy pause. "Simon Newton—
two votes." It was as if the North Pole had spoken.

Simon swirled around in his seat. He could not
believe he had got another vote. Who would dare risk
Miss Ellis's displeasure?

Cybil's hand was in the air. As Simon looked at
her, she grinned and crossed her eyes.

Love washed over him with the force of a tidal

wave. He turned back to the front of the room. He lowered his hand and put it over his chest. He had not known it was possible to love like this.

His eyes blurred. His heart was beating so hard he expected to look down and actually see it pounding, like in cartoons.

He glanced back once again at Cybil Ackerman and knew he would love her until the day he died.

"Simon! *Simon!*"

He looked up. "What?"

"Would you like to tell the class the meaning of the next poem?"

Simon was sitting with his hand on his chest, over the very spot that had pounded so hard years ago. He was surprised to see it was Miss McFawn in front of the class instead of Miss Ellis.

"Would you like to tell the class the meaning of the next poem?" she repeated.

He looked down at the blurred image of his English book. He decided to tell the truth. "No," he said.

Popsickle Legs
and Tub of Blubber

It was after school, and Tony Angotti and Simon were standing at the drinking fountain. Tony had forgotten the insult of being cast as a dill pickle, and he was telling Simon that today was his sister's birthday and he couldn't go home until five o'clock. He began imitating his sister. He could do this perfectly.

"Tony spoils eeeeeverything. He spies on us and he copies what we say. I don't even want to have a partttttttttty if Tony's going to be here. He spoils eeeeeeverything."

He was warming to the imitation when Harriet Haywood came up. "Cybil wants to know if you're mad at her," Harriet said to Simon.

Simon raised his head from the drinking fountain. Before he could answer, Tony asked, "What would he be mad at Ackerman for? What'd she do?"

"*You* know," Harriet said, "for taking his part in the play, for getting to be Ms Indigestion."

"Oh, that." Tony was plainly disappointed. "Well, *is* he mad?"

Simon stood to the side, hand still on the drinking fountain, watching Harriet and Tony Angotti. He felt like a patient being discussed by a doctor and

16

nurse.

"Well, sure he's mad, Haywood," Tony decided. "What'd you think? You think anybody in his right mind wants to be a macaroni pie?"

"A jar of peanut butter," Simon corrected.

"Whatever." Tony warmed to the discussion. "Listen, Haywood, you go back and tell Cybil Ackerman Simon is mad. Tell her he's plenty mad."

"Well, I'll tell her what you said," Harriet began slowly, but Tony cut her off.

"You tell Cybil Ackerman he is so mad he said she ought to be a double popsickle in the play with them legs of hers."

Harriet gasped.

"Wait a minute. I didn't say that."

"Listen, this is between me and Haywood." Tony had recently learned the pleasure of quarrelling with girls and he didn't want to be interrupted.

"I will tell Cybil *exactly* what he said." Harriet's eyes had become smaller. "And don't think I won't either."

She turned so fast it was like a move out of a pro basketball game. She started to walk down the hall. She was so upset over this insult to her best friend's legs that her whole body was trembling.

"And you know what he said about you?" Tony called after her.

She slowed down but did not glance round.

"He said it's too bad there isn't a tub of blubber in the play because that part would be perfect for you!"

17

Simon watched Harriet draw in a breath so deep he thought she was going to inflate herself. "Wait a minute, Harriet," he called. Tony was laughing so hard he had to put one hand on Simon's back to steady himself.

Harriet went directly to the girls' restroom. She pushed the door open with such force that it swung back and forth five times, a school record.

Tony slapped Simon on the back. "I love it," he said. "Old popsickle legs and tub of blubber." Again, he leaned on Simon's back for support.

Simon shrugged him off. The weight of his friend on his back seemed, unexpectedly, enough to send him to his knees. "Get off!"

Tony raised his hands. "I'm—Oh, here she comes, Pal, and she has not forgotten and forgiven."

Harriet came out of the restroom like a missile. There were two girls with her, and the three of them, in tight formation, seemed like an attack force out of *Star Wars*.

Simon and Tony stepped back against the wall to avoid injury. Tony was silenced for a moment and then he stepped back into the middle of the hall as they passed and watched them.

"Hey, Haywood," he called. "You know what Simon just said? He said them girls with you ought to be sacks of potatoes in the play."

The sacks of potatoes stiffened, ruining the tight formation.

"Wait a minute," Simon said. "I didn't say any of

that."

Tony grinned with satisfaction as the girls attempted to go through the school door at the same time. "You can't get three hamburgers in one bun," he called cheerfully. Harriet turned. Her eyes were so slitted with anger that they were invisible.

"Now, I did not say *that*, Harriet," Simon called. "I couldn't have. I—"

"He's just being modest. He thinks of these things and then doesn't want credit. You be sure to tell Ackerman what he said about them legs."

"I will," Harriet called back. She slammed the door and went down the steps.

"She'll tell too," Tony said happily. "She loves to blab. Remember that time I put the trash can upside-down on Miss Ellis's desk and Miss Ellis came in and before she even noticed the trash can, Harriet jumped up and said, 'Tony Angotti did it! Tony Angotti did it!'" He jumped up and down on the pavement to demonstrate. Then he said, "Course I don't have the flab she's got. When Haywood jumps up and down, windows all over the school slam shut."

"Why do you—" Simon began, but Tony interrupted.

"And then came victory. Miss Ellis said, 'What did Tony do?' And then she notices that there is a trash can upside-down on her desk. Oh, horrors! And before anyone can stop her, she picks up the trash can and trash falls all over her desk!"

In the silence that followed Tony's laughter,

Simon asked his question again. "Why do you do stuff like that?"

"Like what?"

"Lie!"

"Oh," he said, shrugging. "Everybody in my family lies. You know that."

"Well, quit lying about me!"

"Even my mom lies. The first thing she ever said to me that I can remember was a lie. She told me chocolate-covered cherries were medicine."

"That's different, Tony. That's—"

"My mom would make a real bad face every time she ate one. It took me three, four years before I'd even try a chocolate-covered cherry. She also told me that if I made ugly faces my face would freeze like that and that if I sat too close to the TV I wouldn't be able to see anything but black and white."

Tony Angotti went on, happily listing his mother's lies. Simon walked beside him in silence. His long friendship with Tony, which had brought him such pleasure in the early grades, seemed this year to be bringing him only discomfort. He walked slower. He had the uneasy feeling that he had been led, half-willingly, like a blinded horse, into a stream and abandoned. And now, blindfold lifted, he had to face the current alone.

"And my grandmother—talk about lies! My grandmother told me that if I wore my cousin Bennie's shoes—which were two sizes too little—see, we were out in Wheeling and my uncle died and we all had to go to the funeral and I didn't have any dark shoes. So she told me that if I wore my cousin Bennie's shoes, something nice would happen because they were magic shoes. Can you believe that! And I put them on—can you believe *that?* And off I go to the funeral in my magic shoes—I could barely walk." He began to limp comically. "The toes were pointy, Simon—they were like real little old men's shoes!"

Simon smiled despite himself.

"And when I got home, I had blisters, them things were that big and my grandmother—you know what she told me? She told me they were magic blisters and that if I didn't pop them, they would turn into silver dollars!"

"Did you pop them?" Simon asked.

"No!—well, yes, but only after Annette laughed at me. Anyway, *that* was lying." Pride in the family trait showed in his face and voice. "I could never think of anything that good."

Simon glanced at him and then back at his own feet, dragging along in his torn sneakers. His smile faded. "Yes, but you're just getting started," he predicted in a low voice.

"That's true." Tony nodded. "That is sooooo true."

Let My Dad Kidnap Me

Simon entered the house and sighed with relief at being rid of Tony. Then he picked up the mail.

When there was a letter from his father—and there had only been four—he felt worse. In the first two letters, his father was living on a boat off the coast of California; in the next two, in a forest in Oregon. The letters were Robinson Crusoe descriptions of what he was eating and how he gathered wood and built fires and mended his clothes.

The letters made Simon hate the outdoors in the way he would hate a rival. And it seemed to Simon that Nature had sensed his hate, just as a dog senses fear, and had sent poison ivy and wasps and pollen to retaliate.

He could imagine a Mother Nature who had thought up hurricanes and tornadoes pointing in his direction, instructing her plants and insects with a smile. "Sickum!"

Today there was no letter. I should stop hoping for letters, he told himself. It was as useless as trying to get kidnapped in second grade. He had finally learned to smile about that now.

It was the first awful winter without his father and

Simon had seen a TV special about a father who had left, just like his father, and then the father had come back and kidnapped his own son!

The idea had almost made Simon stop breathing. Maybe at this very moment—the possibility made him put his hand on his chest, right over his pounding heart—maybe at this very moment his father was planning to kidnap him.

It was like suddenly learning there's Christmas or television. There's kidnapping.

It was odd. He could remember how in first grade they had had long lessons on the dangers of being kidnapped. Mr Repokis had given them an oral quiz about it.

"Now if someone offered you an ice-cream sundae with marshmallows, nuts, bananas *and* decorettes, would you get in the car with them?"

"Noooooooo."

"And if someone offered to give you a Barbie doll with a majorette suit and a light-up baton, would you get in the car with them?"

"Nooooooooo."

"And if someone offered to give you a Matchbox car with real headlights and a real engine, would you get in the car with them?"

They were all collecting Matchbox cars then, and Bennie Hoffman, overcome, had cried, "*I* would!" and they had to start all over again, because kidnapping was such a terrible thing.

Now it became Simon's dream. Let my dad kidnap

me, he prayed as he played dangerously near the road at recess. Let my dad kidnap me, he pleaded as he stood at the edge of the driveway. Let my dad kidnap me, he begged as he slowly passed a strange van parked down the street.

He was always at the edge of the street in those days, waiting for the feel of his father's arm as he was lifted into the waiting van and driven away.

It was December before he finally gave up. It was such a cold month that his mother would not let him sit outside without his Yogi Bear face mask. Even he, with all his dreams, had to admit that it was unlikely he would be kidnapped in that attire.

A voice at the door said, "I forgot. I can't go home till after the parttttty." It was Tony, speaking in his sister Annette's voice.

"I'll come out," Simon said quickly, but before he could open the door, Tony was inside.

Tony came through the house like a pickpocket, opening drawers, picking up objects, glancing in envelopes, pulling out letters. He paused to glance through the Newtons' mail.

"Nothing from your old man?"

"No."

Tony looked with interest at a Reader's Digest Sweepstakes Entry. "He must not have got his head together yet," he commented.

"No."

"Do you mind if I take this? I'd like to win some of this stuff—that boat, for instance."

"There's no lake around here."

"Well, do you mind if I take it?"

"No!" He paused, then said calmly, "Let's go outside."

They went out and sat on the steps. Tony put his Sweepstakes Entry in his back pocket. "It's not fair," he said. "Why am I—a member of the family—kept out of my own home so that strangers can come in and eat cake?"

"Because you imitate your sister and her friends and spy on them," Simon answered with unusual bluntness.

"Come on. When did I spy?"

"Last week."

"Name two other times." He broke off and sighed. "Oh, never mind." Suddenly he straightened. "Hey, here comes Haywood. What's the Tub doing walking past your house?"

"Don't call her that. Maybe she's on her way somewhere. Lay off, will you?"

"Huh, she's walking past your house for one reason. She wants to see you."

"After what you said this afternoon, I would be the last person she'd want to see."

"Listen, I know about walking past people's houses. My sister Annette does it all the time. When she wants to see Rickie Wurts, she walks past his house, reallllll slow, just like Haywood's doing. Sometimes she pretends to be looking for something she's lost. That way she can walk past ten, fifteen times until he comes out of the house." He broke off to yell, "Haywood, where are you going?"

Harriet turned her head and looked surprised to see them. Then she exhaled, giving the impression that the two of them were giving off an unpleasant odour.

"Come on," Tony said. He grabbed Simon's shirt and pulled him down the sidewalk to where Harriet was waiting at the edge of the street.

"Well, I didn't expect to see *you*," Harriet said. She lowered her eyes with the coldness of someone recently called a tub of blubber.

"It's his house," Tony said. "Why wouldn't you expect to see him?"

"I just thought," she was colder than ever now, "that after what you said today, the two of you would have the decency to stay out of my way."

"We want to stay out of your way, Haywood," Tony said, "only how are we going to do that when you come looking for us?"

"I was *not* looking for you!"

"She wasn't looking for us, Tony," Simon said.

"Listen, I know what's happening here. I've got experience in these things." Tony put up his hands. "Okay, Haywood, so while you weren't looking for us, what were you going to tell us when you found us?"

"Nothing, except that I told Cybil what you said about her legs."

Harriet was glancing from Simon to Tony now,

including them both in the responsibility for the insult.

"Well, I'm glad to hear that, Haywood," Tony said. "You keep things like that to yourself, you'll end up in the funny farm."

"And you know what she said about you?" She was looking right at Tony Angotti now, but Simon felt she was talking about him too.

"No, I don't know what Popsickle Legs said about us and I don't want to know."

Simon said, "I do."

Suddenly Harriet hesitated. She glanced from Tony to Simon. Simon could see that she wanted to tell them, indeed, she had walked all the way over here to tell them, but his eagerness made her change her mind.

"I'm not going to tell you," she said and started walking away.

Tony yelled, "Haywood, you mean you come all the way over here to see us, walk fifteen, twenty blocks, and we take pity on you and come down from the porch and then you won't tell us what Cybil said?"

"You've got it," Harriet said over her shoulder.

Simon and Tony watched her until she turned the corner. Then Tony said in a surprised voice, "I wonder what Cybil did say about us."

"I don't know."

"It had to be an insult of some kind."

"Of course."

27

"But there's nothing to insult!" He held out both hands to show he was hiding no flaws.

"Well, we're not perfect," Simon said.

Tony was silent while he went over a mental checklist of his body. "Really, there's nothing to insult!"

"Maybe she said we're lousy baseball players."

"What kind of insult is that? We call her legs popsickle sticks and she comes up with, 'Well, you play poor baseball.' Come on, if I know Cybil Ackerman, she said something a lot worse than that."

"Yes, she could."

Tony stood for a moment, looking up the street where Harriet had disappeared. Then he turned abruptly and said, "I'm going home."

"It's not five o'clock yet. Annette's party isn't over. You . . ."

"Right. I've got . . ." he checked his watch . . . "exactly twenty minutes to spoil eeeeeverything." He started down the sidewalk for home, then he turned. "And I'll let you know tomorrow what Ackerman said about us."

Tears and Ravioli

Simon went back into the house and looked in the kitchen. His mother sometimes left notes for him. "Put the casserole in the oven. Clean the celery." Today the message was "Defrost the chicken." He took the package from the freezer. He was like a robot kitchen helper, he sometimes thought, who performed acts without understanding what he was doing.

He went back to the living-room. The television was broken so he sat doing nothing, hands dangling at his sides.

Simon and Tony were known as best friends. Their friendship had been sealed in second grade when the entire class was asked to write essays on their fathers.

Simon refused to write one, and Tony could not because his father had died when he was one year old. Tony could not even remember his father. So they had sat in their desks, both miserable, both staring at their dirty fingernails while other children went to the front of the room and read happily, "My father is a dentist. He plays golf. He plays tennis. He has a new car."

When the voting was held on the best paper—Billy

Bonfili won because his father was the high school football coach—only Simon and Tony did not vote.

"You don't have a father?" Tony asked after school. He had waited at the door to ask this, his long face intent.

"I have one," Simon said carefully, "but he's gone."

"Where?"

"I don't know."

"I had one but he's dead."

"Oh."

And thus sealed together by a mutual loss rather than mutual interest, their friendship had begun. They walked together to Tony's house.

"Do you like ravioli?" Tony asked at the edge of the driveway.

"I don't know."

"You've never had ravioli?"

"No."

"Well, come *on!*"

They went into Tony's house, and Simon sat at the kitchen table. He watched while Tony heated the ravioli. He was looking down at his steaming plate, at the strange, soft squares, when Tony's grandfather came in.

"You want some ravioli, Pap-pap?" Tony asked at the stove.

Pap-pap nodded, pulled out his chair, sat heavily. When the three of them were seated, plates full, Tony said, "He doesn't have a father either."

Pap-pap looked over at Simon. His eyes, blue as a baby's, began to fill with tears. "You got no papa?"

"I have one but he's gone."

Pap-pap pulled out his handkerchief. It was old and faded because it was used all the time. "Your papa left home?" he asked.

"Yes."

"He comes to visit?"

"No."

"He writes?"

"We had one letter."

"One letter," Pap-pap said sadly. He shook his head. Tears spilled on to his wrinkled cheeks. He wiped his eyes and blew his nose.

"He cries a lot," Tony explained to Simon.

Simon nodded. He looked from Tony to the weeping Pap-pap. Simon had not seen his mother cry when his father left. He himself had not cried. And here, across the table, from an old man he had never seen before, were tears for his father. He felt the first stirring of tears in his own eyes.

"Sometimes he cries just because the moon's full, you know, because it's beautiful," Tony explained as he chewed. "And sometimes he cries because he sees a picture that reminds him of home and sometimes—well, he just cries all the time. It doesn't mean anything."

Simon nodded again.

"That's not true," Pap-pap said. "It means something." He peered at them over his handkerchief. "It means I get so full, I spill over." He made a gesture with his handkerchief as if it were water pouring over a dam. Then he wiped his cheeks again, and, sniffling, began to eat.

Simon ducked his head, cut a piece of ravioli in half with his fork and put it in his mouth. The tears in his own eyes, the tightening of his throat made him unable to swallow, but there was something in the soft warm food, the weeping sympathetic man across the table that would make him feel sentimental every time he ate ravioli. Even in the school cafeteria, where ravioli came straight from a can, he would feel tears in his eyes when he ate.

Simon got up and went back into the kitchen. He opened the refrigerator. His mother's taste ran to yoghurt and natural foods and fresh vegetables and bran muffins. He selected a cup of yoghurt and ate it slowly with a spoon, feeling nothing at all.

Then he went back into the living-room, sat in his same seat and turned his thoughts to Cybil Ackerman.

At Cybil Ackerman's House

Cybil Ackerman was practising the piano. This was
so that she could play trumpet in the band when she
got to junior high school. It was a deal she had made
with her father. She was playing intently, eyes dart-
ing from the music to her hands. There was a carrot
in her mouth. The doorbell rang.

"Cybil, open the door please," Mrs Ackerman
called.

Cybil removed the carrot from her mouth and
stuck it in a jar of peanut butter beside her music.
"I'm practising," she called back.

"Cynthia?"

"I'm studying."

"Clara?"

"I'm in the bathroom."

There was a rule in the Ackerman house that
whoever was least busy had to answer the door and
the phone. Mrs Ackerman made the decision.
"Cybil."

"Oh, all right." Cybil got up. "But I was just
about to get that part."

She dipped her carrot into the peanut butter as she
went to the door. She saw through the screen that

Tony Angotti was standing on the porch. His hands were in his pockets. A slight smile of anticipation was on his face.

"Who is it?" Clara and Cynthia both called.

"Nobody!" Cybil called back.

Tony Angotti shifted.

"What do you want?" Cybil asked. She took a bite of peanut-butter-covered carrot.

"Nothing. I was just passing by, and I figured I'd find out what you said about Simon. *I* don't want to know but he—well, you know how *he* is—he . . ."

"I didn't say anything about Simon." Crunch, crunch. "I like Simon."

"Well, sure, but after Harriet told you he said you had popsickle legs . . ."

"I do have popsickle legs."

"No." The conversation was not going as Tony had anticipated. "I mean Harriet said you said something bad about Simon and maybe," he gave an improbable laugh, "about me."

"Oh, I said you were juvenile."

"What?" He leaned forward as if he had been struck a light blow on the back of the neck.

"Juvenile," she repeated.

"Me juvenile? Or Simon?"

"You."

"Who's at the door, Cybil?" Mrs Ackerman called.

"Nobody."

"Then get back to your practising."

34

"That's what I'm trying to do!"

Tony said, "But why would you say that about me?" He was genuinely puzzled. "Simon's the one who acts like he's still in kindergarten. If I told you some of the stupid stuff he does, you wouldn't believe me. One time he . . ."

"I've got to go."

"Wait a minute, Cybil, give me a chance. Just let me tell you one stupid thing that Simon Newton did, just one thing and then you can decide which of us is juvenile."

Cybil sighed, stuck her carrot in the peanut butter jar and waited.

"Okay, Simon was going to this funeral, see. His uncle died while he was visiting his grandmother and he didn't have any dark shoes. And so his grand-mother told him that his cousin Bennie's shoes were magic shoes, and that if he wore them something good would happen. And so, believe it or not, he puts on the magic shoes and limps off to the funeral. They were two sizes too little, they were like tiny little men's shoes and . . ."

Clara stuck her head around the door to see who was on the porch. "Mom," she called, "Cybil's talk-ing to a boy! And if she can talk to a boy before she finishes practising then I can talk to Tommy before I finish studying. Tommy's been sitting in the garage for fifteen minutes and—"

"Girls!" Mrs Ackerman warned.

"I was not talking to a *boy*," Cybil explained, "I

35

was talking to Tony Angotti!"

As Cybil turned away and shut the door on him and his unfinished story, Tony Angotti could see that she was grinning at her sister and that her eyes were crossed.

In the Bushes

Simon Newton heard this conversation from the bushes where he happened to be hiding.

That night, after supper, he had decided to walk over to Cybil's house. He would just walk up the sidewalk slowly, perhaps pretending to have lost something and then, when Cybil came out of the house he would tell her that it was Tony, not he, who had thought up the unfortunate similarity between her legs and popsickle sticks. "I like straight legs," he would tell her.

He would then go on to say that he was glad she was going to be Ms Indigestion. This was true. Now that he had had a chance to realistically imagine himself in costume, his peanut butter sign and his one line—"I am rich in protein and blah—blah—blah—" did seem like a reprieve from public humiliation.

He was going over this in his mind, practising it, when he turned the corner and saw Cybil's house.

Simon had walked past Cybil's house many times since that Arbor Day when he fell in love with her, and he never tired of doing so. Cybil had four sisters—all had red curly hair and looked alike, and so he had the pleasure when the youngest—Clarice—

came running out, of seeing what Cybil had looked like in first grade. And when the oldest—Cynthia—came out, of seeing what Cybil would look like in high school.

Tonight, for the first time, when he looked at Cybil's house, he got a nasty shock. Tony Angotti was standing on the porch. Tony Angotti was ringing the bell and straightening his jacket. Tony Angotti was smirking.

Keeping low, Simon had made his way behind the hedge, up to the shrubbery, and behind the bushes to the side of the porch. He had been here before too. Once he had sneaked up to look in the window so he could see what Cybil's living-room looked like, and at that exact moment Mrs Ackerman had come out to cut some oleanders for a party she was having. Simon had crouched there, head against his knees, heart throbbing, sweat running down his legs, while Mrs Ackerman snipped blossoms around his head with a pair of shears.

This time he crouched in place just in time to hear Cybil ask, "What do you want?" and to hear the crunch of her carrot. And now, only minutes later, with every word of the conversation between Cybil and Tony burning in his brain, he watched through the leaves as Tony Angotti made his way down the driveway.

Simon was stunned by what he had heard. "Simon's the one who acts like he's still in kindergarten . . . Just let me tell you one stupid thing that

Simon did . . . Simon was going to this funeral, see . . ."

A funny lie—that was how he thought of Tony's attributing the tub of blubber and sack of potatoes similes to him—a funny lie was one thing. He had survived dozens of those over the years. What he had just heard was character assassination. He could sue.

Simon watched with slitted eyes as Tony paused at the edge of the street. Simon was breathing through his mouth, the way he did when the pollen was bad.

Tony lifted his head as the opening notes of "Under the Golden Eagle" floated through the window. He scratched his head, a sure sign of thought. He adjusted his jacket. He turned his face towards the window as alert as a listening bird.

Tony Angotti was having a hard time believing that Cybil had called him juvenile. Him, Tony Angotti, who looked like Donny Osmond! He paused, head turned to the music, trying to find an answer.

Tony's head shifted with another thought. Tony could not keep his head still when he was thinking. Sometimes during a science test, his head would snap up as quickly as if he had a sudden toothache.

Cybil Ackerman was trying to make him jealous by pretending to like Simon Newton who, everyone knew, really was juvenile! That was it! At this very moment, Tony thought, she was probably watching him through the window.

39

He turned. With studied nonchalance, he made his way to the hedge. Quickly, head low, he ducked behind the hedge and walked in a crouch to the bushes. Holding his hands over his face to protect it from scratches, he squirmed through the bushes to a place beneath the window. Cautiously he lifted his head.

Simon watched all this with an awful fascination. Seeing Tony come closer and closer, knowing a showdown here in the bushes was inevitable, he still made no effort to get away or hide. He waited, his eyes bright with anger.

Tony straightened and peered into the window. His face reflected his disappointment. His mouth hung open.

He had somehow expected to see Cybil Ackerman standing behind the curtain, peering out, trying to see him as he walked away. That was what Annette did when Rickie Wurts left. Instead here she was, playing the piano with a carrot stuck in her mouth.

It was hard for Tony to believe. Cybil Ackerman was not even pretty. Her legs really were like popsickle sticks.

And yet here she was treating him, Tony Angotti, the image of Donny Osmond, as if he were an ordinary person. No, worse—as if he were nothing. He was glad no one was round to see this humiliation.

"Cybil!"

One of Cybil's sisters rushed into the living-room. Cybil's hands stopped playing, hovered over the keys.

"Quick, play 'The Wedding March' while Clara goes down the steps to meet Tommy. Hurry, she's leaving."

"I don't know the music."

"Fake it!"

Cybil's hand twitched, hesitated, then struck.

Dum da-da-da. Dum da-da-de. Dum da-da-daaaaaaaaa-da-da dadadadada-deeeeeee.

"Cybil! Cynthia! That's not funny!" Clara yelled. She spun around on the porch and glared back at the open window.

Tony Angotti crouched so quickly his knees popped. He bowed like a Moslem.

Clara waited, eyes on the window, until she was sure Cybil was through with "The Wedding March". Then, as the laboured strains of "Under the Golden Eagle" floated through the window again, she went down the steps to where Tommy was waiting.

"Excuse my sisters," she said, "they think they're soooooo funny."

Tony Angotti lifted his head. He brushed dirt from his brow. He pulled his T-shirt from his stomach where it had stuck with his sweat. He was now doubly grateful that no one could see him here on his knees.

It was then that he turned his head and saw Simon Newton.

The Spies and the Lies

"I didn't know you went around hiding in the bushes, spying on your friends," Tony Angotti said as soon as they were safely on the sidewalk. After that one long, hard moment in the oleanders when their eyes met and locked, they had not glanced at each other. They were now walking, eyes down, towards Simon's house.

"May I point out", Simon said, "that you were in the same bushes?"

They kept walking. Each was torn by the feeling that the other's crime was worse, and yet unable to put that proof into words.

"That doesn't count," Tony said. "I had a reason."

"Maybe I had a reason too."

There was a silence, awkward and long, while each searched for another accusation. Then Simon brushed his hair from his forehead and said with a faint smile, "Anyway, did you find out what Cybil said about you?"

"You didn't hear?"

"No," he lied, "I got there right after that."

"You didn't hear what she said?"

"No."

Tony glanced at Simon, quickly, then away. "Well, she didn't say anything about me, Pal. She said you were juvenile."

"What?"

"You heard me—juvenile." Tony would like to have spelled the word out for emphasis, but he wasn't sure if it started with a "j" or "g".

"Oh."

Tony sighed, partly from relief, partly from being on safe territory—lying. "I tried to tell her you weren't, but she wouldn't listen. Right in the middle of a long story about you—I was really pouring it on—she just went back in the house."

"What story were you telling?"

"About the time you broke your arm," he said swiftly, happy he came from a family where lying was an inborn gift. "And that when they set it you didn't take any ether and . . ."

"I never broke my arm."

"Oh, I thought you did. Well, anyway, she wouldn't listen. She went in the house and started playing the piano. You heard that?"

Simon nodded. "Well, I've got to go in."

"Sure."

Their eyes met again, a questioning look, but both of them turned away before anything was revealed. Tony kept watching Simon as Simon walked up the steps. Then he shrugged. "Ahh!" He made the motion of pushing Simon and the whole stupid business away as he turned to go home.

"Did you and Tony have a fight?" Simon's mother asked as he came in the door.

"Why do you ask that?"

"Because you always have that look on your face when you have a fight."

"I don't have any 'look' on my face."

"Yes, you do. Your face gets red and . . ."

"Maybe I've been running. Maybe I've been in the sun." He resented the fact that his emotions showed on his face. "Just leave me alone."

He was aware that his mother was watching him closely. Ever since his father left, she had been doing this. How are you? How do you feel? Is there anything wrong? Talk to me. It was as if she never wanted to be taken by surprise again.

"I'm not going to run away and live in a forest, if that's what you're thinking," he had said once in exasperation. "May I remind you of my allergies and my magnetic ability to attract wasps?"

"I know you're not going to run away," she'd said, but the fact that he'd put the thought into words only seemed to make her worry more.

"Simon . . ."

"Oh, leave me alone," he said again. He sometimes had the feeling that when he died, if people would just leave him alone, he could come back to life.

She sighed and smiled. "Then tell me what *isn't*

44

wrong, tell me something, anything."

He paused, his red face turned towards the blank television set. The TV had broken three months ago, during a re-run of "Bonanza", Simon's favourite serial, and Mrs Newton had not had it repaired. From habit, Simon still watched the blank screen when he wanted to be diverted.

"Tell me something that happened at school to-day," she suggested.

He looked at her. "And then I can go to my room?"

"Yes, *if* it's about you. Don't tell me about some-body throwing up in the cafeteria."

"That happened yesterday. Well, let's see. Oh, here's the big news of today. We are having a nutri-tion play. This is because Miss McFawn used to teach first grade where they did nothing but put on plays. I have been selected for a lesser role—the peanut butter, but I shall try to bring dignity and character to the part. Can I go?"

"What's Tony?"

His face did not change expression. "Dill pickle."

"Go on."

"Well, that's basically it. One of the green beans—Laura Goode—hit me because I laughed when Tony said she actually resembled a green bean from the side."

"Aw."

"*Hard*, Mom. Look." He found a small bruise above his elbow and showed it to her. "And then I

45

was falsely accused of calling two other girls sacks of potatoes and one girl a tub of blubber which, incidentally, she does resemble. The tub of blubber did not hit me, fortunately, or I would be in hospital."

He looked at her, keeping his face bright and cheerful so she would know he was fine and leave him alone. "Is that enough?"

"Yes."

"Can I go now?"

"Simon, you are not a prisoner. I just like you to tell me things."

"That's all there is to tell."

As he left the room she called after him. "Simon."

"What?"

"Don't let Tony take advantage of you."

He stopped where he stood. He sighed with irritation. "That is not the problem."

"What is the problem, then?"

His shoulders sagged. With his back to her he said, "Everything is just so complicated."

"How?" she asked quickly, sitting forward on the edge of the sofa.

Fathers desert you, he told himself, friends lie about you, teachers humiliate you—and those are supposed to be the good guys. He sighed. "Oh, nothing," he said.

"I *want* to know."

"Forget I said anything."

He went into his room and shut the door. As he

flopped down on the bed he remembered that was something his father used to say, "Everything's just got so damn complicated."

Good Things/Bad Things

That night as Simon lay in bed he decided to try and think of the good things about Tony Angotti. This was because he now hated Tony so much he could not understand why they had ever been friends. He also, at this point, wanted to conceal from Tony how he felt and that now seemed impossible, not unless his hatred was somehow diluted.

He started thinking as soon as he got into bed and it was ten o'clock before he thought of the first thing.

<u>Good Thing No. 1</u>

At times Tony Angotti would say the right thing. Like, one time in third grade, he and Tony decided to bore a small hole in the school wall. Tony was in room 104 that year and Simon was in 106. It was the first year they had been separated and they wanted this hole so they could pass secret code messages to each other.

Simon brought a drill from home, hidden under his jacket, and during recess they began to work on the hole. Just when Simon was getting started, Mrs Albertson came in.

"What are you doing?" she asked. She was right behind Simon.

He was so startled that he dropped the drill. Mrs Albertson picked it up.

"Boring a hole," he stammered.

Just then Mrs Albertson and Simon heard a tapping on the wall. Simon knew it was Tony Angotti, directing the drill so the hole wouldn't go through the blackboard.

Mrs Albertson walked out into the hall and down to room 104. There was Tony, waiting to see the drill come through. He was so excited that he didn't see Mrs Albertson until she touched his shoulder. Then he screamed.

"Come with me," she said.

She sat them down and gave them a talk about respecting school property and made them promise not to drill any more holes. They promised even before she finished the sentence. When they were leaving the room, Tony turned and said, "Could we have his drill back? It's borrowed."

"After school," Mrs Albertson said.

Only a good friend, Simon reminded himself, would have asked about the drill.

Simon had no sooner thought of this when, against his will, he remembered a bad thing.

One time in second grade Tony told Miss Ellis that Simon had licked the icing off one of the Christmas cupcakes when he had only pretended to do that to be funny, and then Miss Ellis had made him take the cupcake that looked like it had been licked!

It was ten-thirty before Simon was able to think of

another good thing about Tony Angotti.

Good Thing No. 2

At times Tony Angotti could be nice.

Like one day Simon was over at Tony's house and Pap-pap was crying. This day everybody was busy and so nobody was paying any attention to him.

Finally Tony's mother said, "Tony, go and see what's wrong with Pap-pap."

"Why can't Annette do it? I've got company."

"Who?"

He pointed to Simon.

"Go and see about Pap-pap." Mrs Angotti raised her hand. Mrs Angotti had a ring with a stone as big as a bird's egg, and she could—Tony claimed—thump you on the head with it from ten feet away.

"All right!" Tony got up and backed out of the room.

He and Simon went outside and sat on the bench by Pap-pap, who was crying harder now, wiping his eyes with an old faded handkerchief.

"Is anything wrong?" Tony asked.

Pap-pap shook his head.

"Do you hurt?"

Again Pap-pap shook his head.

"Well, I'm supposed to find out what's wrong!"

At last Pap-pap managed to speak. "I've got too good a memory, that's my trouble."

"What?"

He mopped his eyes. "I was standing by the fence, see, over there by the bushes, and I smelled my mama's apron."

"What?"

"I used to be a puny little kid, see, and the big kids would pick on me and I would run home crying and hide my face in my mama's apron. I never forgot the way her apron smelled." He started crying again. "Over there." He waved with his handkerchief. "Over there, that's my mama's apron."

"Show me," Tony said in a nice voice.

The three of them got up and walked over to the fence. They stood there in a gush of warm air. Simon realized they were standing by the vent from the Angottis' stove and Mrs Angotti was cooking peppers in olive oil.

"That's it?" Tony asked.

Pap-pap wiped his eyes, nodding.

"Nice," Tony said, breathing deeply.

Pap-pap nodded again, smiling a little now, happy to be sharing the smell of his mama's apron with them. Simon was smiling a little himself.

And the three of them stood there together, inhaling, until Mrs Angotti had finished frying peppers.

Then again, right away, Simon remembered another bad thing about Tony Angotti.

When they were in first grade they used to play the game Simon Says on rainy days. Since Simon was the only student named Simon, Mr Repokis let him start the game a lot. Those were his happiest moments in first grade.

"Simon says, 'Stoop down,'" he'd yell, as happy as a dictator. "Simon says, 'Hands on your ears.'" He could have gone on like that for hours.

Then one day, after one of his best games in which even Wanda Sanchez had been tricked, Tony said, "You should stop doing that."

"What?"

"Leading that stupid game."

"Why?" Simon had been genuinely surprised. He had thought he was the envy of the class.

"Because you lisp."

"What?"

"You lisp!" he said. "Thimon thays thtoop down!"

"That's—that's because of my teeth," he said, both lisping and stuttering now.

"Well, it still makes you look *thtupid*!"

After that, Simon did not try to think of any more nice things about Tony Angotti.

T-Bone's Invitation

Cybil's sister Clarice was out on the roof of the porch. She had been there twenty minutes, sitting like a Hindu, facing out over the front yard.

"Come in off the roof, Clarice," Mrs Ackerman called.

"I'm not coming in until Cybil apologizes for calling me Boney!"

"Cybil!"

"Well, Mom, she *is* boney and you told us always to be truthful."

"Cybil!"

"All right, all right. I apologize . . ."

Clarice got up and crawled to the window. As her foot went over the sill, Cybil added, ". . . to *Skinny!*"

Clarice bounced back on to the porch roof. "Mom, now she's calling me Skinny!"

"Cybil!"

"Listen, Mom, she's on the roof and you told us we couldn't play on the roof because it made us look like the monkey house at the zoo."

"Cybil!"

"All right! I apologize to *Glamorous!*"

"That's more like it." Clarice began climbing in

the window again.

Cybil started to say something else, but she caught sight of Simon across the street. "Oh, Simon, wait a minute. Don't go away. I'm coming out."

Simon had been standing beneath a tree, in the shadows, watching the house. He had intended to walk by slowly, pretending to have lost something, but he had become so interested in the sight of Clarice sitting on the roof that he had forgotten his plan.

He waited dutifully until Cybil came running out of the house. "Guess what? Harriet's having a pet show and she wants you to come and bring your dog."

"T-Bone?"

"Yes."

Simon was caught by surprise by the invitation; he knew Harriet would not want him at anything other than a hanging.

"T-Bone's not much for shows," he said.

"That doesn't matter."

"And also I don't think Harriet would want me to come. She has it in her mind that I called her a—well, that I called her something unattractive."

"A tub of blubber?"

"Yes."

"She's forgotten about that."

"I don't think so. I know the sacks of potatoes haven't. They keep hitting me with their books in the hall."

"I *want* you to come."

He hesitated, decided to level with her. "My dog—look, we got him at the pound. And the day mom and I went over there, well, it was on a Friday and they put all the dogs that are left to sleep on Saturday and he was the only dog left." He swallowed. "So we didn't choose him, you know, because he was real beautiful or cute or spotted or anything like that. We chose him because he was left."

"But I like dogs that are just dogs. I want him to come. And, listen, there's a prize for the best costume. He could win that."

Simon shook his head. If T-Bone was anything like him—and Simon often felt the kinship—then he wouldn't want to wear a costume either.

"I want you to come. Tony's coming."

His head snapped up. "Tony Angotti?"

"Yes."

"Tony doesn't even have a dog."

"He's going to borrow his aunt's poodle, and it can pop balloons and open its own Gainesburgers and say its prayers. Guess what its name is?"

Simon shook his head.

"Miss Vicki!" She grinned and crossed her eyes.

Normally this would have turned his knees to jelly, but the news about Tony alarmed him.

"When did you see Tony?" he asked.

"Just about fifteen minutes ago. He was walking by the house looking for something he'd lost."

"Oh."

"At first I said, 'No.' You can't *borrow* a pet, because somebody could go out and *borrow* Lassie and win all the prizes. But he said it was a *family* dog that belonged to the whole family, so anyway he's coming and he thinks Miss Vicki can win Best Behaved and Best Costume and Best Trick. I suppose I shouldn't give this away, but guess what Miss Vicki's costume's going to be?"

"I don't know."

"A baby cap and diaper!"

There was a pause while she grinned. In the pause Simon said, "You know, I believe I will come to the pet show. If Tony's going to be there—I mean, well, if my *friend's* going to be there, I want to be there too."

"Great! It's tomorrow afternoon at two o'clock."

"T-Bone and I will be there."

The Love Quiz

Simon walked to Tony's house with his face set. He was furious. He felt somehow like a character in that fairy tale where the little pigs tell the wolf to meet them at six o'clock and then they go at five and get all the apples. He had no idea what he would do when he actually saw Tony, but he knew he had to confront him.

He rang the bell, and waited.

"Come on in. I want to show you something," Tony said. He pulled Simon in by the shirt.

"I understand you were over at Cybil's this morning, that you *lost* something and were looking for it," Simon said in a voice carefully drained of emotion.

"I didn't *lose* anything. I was doing an errand for my mom, and Cybil comes running out on them popsickle legs of hers. 'Wait a minute, Tonn-nnnnnny.' Guess what she wanted? She wanted me to come to a pet show. I said, 'I ain't got no pet.' She said, 'Borrow one.' I thought she was going to get down on her knees so I finally said, 'All right, I'll borrow my aunt's poodle.' Come on."

He looked both ways and then slipped into his sister's room. "I've got to show you this," he said.

"What is it?"

"It's a quiz—a love quiz—you do it to find out if you're in love."

"Why would you be doing a quiz like that?" Simon asked in the same flat voice.

"*I'm* not doing it. It's my sister. Annette's doing it to find out if she's in love with—guess who?"

"I don't know."

"Bubsie Frasure!" He laughed. "Bubsie Frasure—you know he led our school patrol last year. If we got out of line, he'd stamp his foot? Well, look at this. You'll love it, Simon. Question One: Do you think about this person (a) occasionally (b) often (c) most of the time (d) all of the time?" He looked at Simon. "And, Simon, my sister—I'm ashamed to tell you this—my sister has ticked (d). My sister thinks about Bubsie Frasure *all of the time*."

Simon sighed.

"Simon, all the time! That don't leave room for arithmetic, nuclear energy, world affairs—nothing!"

He shook his head in disbelief. "Question Two: When you are not with this person you are (a) happy (b) content (c) unhappy (d) miserable. My sister once again has gone for the big D. Simon, she is *miserable* when she's . . ." Suddenly he lowered the notebook. "Hey, want to spy on them?"

"No."

"They're on the back porch. We just have to crawl into the living-room and hide under the picture window. Come on."

Tony gave Simon a tug on his T-shirt and they left the room. Simon, eyes cold and unsmiling, followed. They crouched beneath the window in time to hear this conversation:

Annette: What are you thinking about, Bubsie?

Bubsie: Nothing.

Annette: Really, what are you thinking about?

Bubsie: Nothing!

Annette (getting kind of desperate): But they say we're always thinking of something.

Bubsie: Even when we're asleep?

Annette: Yes, isn't that wild?

Bubsie: Then I guess I must be thinking of something.

Annette: What?

Tony punched Simon to get his attention. Then he grinned a Groucho Marx grin and crossed his eyes.

Bubsie: I guess I was thinking about what I'm going to be doing tomorrow.

Annette: What are you going to do tomorrow?

Bubsie: Oh, just mess around.

The conversation on the porch continued, but Simon did not hear it. He was stunned. He had never seen Tony Angotti cross his eyes before. He had never known he could cross his eyes—and Tony was not one to keep a talent like that hidden for four years. He felt confused, suspicious, betrayed. His face started to burn.

"Let's go. This is boring." Tony mouthed the words.

They straightened, walked into the hall and through the kitchen. Simon stumbled over the doorstep and on to the porch in time to hear Annette say, "Bubsie, what are you thinking about *now*?"

"I have to go," Simon said quickly. He did not look at Tony. He knew all his emotions—even the ones he didn't understand—would be revealed in his red face. Then he added defiantly, "I'm going to the pet show too and I have to find a costume for T-Bone."

"You're taking T-Bone to the pet show?"

"Yes."

"*T-Bone?*"

"Yes!"

"No offence, Pal, but T-Bone—unless they're giving a prize for the dog who looks like he swallowed the most rotten bird—well, he hasn't got a prayer."

"I'll see you there," Simon said. He kept his hands in his pockets so he would not smash Tony Angotti in the face.

The Pirate

"What on earth are you doing?" Simon's mother asked from the doorway.

He jumped as if he had been caught committing a crime. "Nothing," he said quickly. He snatched the pirate's hat from T-Bone's head and attempted to hide the eye-patch under his knee.

"Are you making a costume for the dog?" she asked. She moved into the room.

"What if I am?" he said, trying for dignity.

"Well, it just seems so odd. I cannot imagine *you* making a dog costume."

"We're going to a pet show," he said calmly. He waited, hoping she would go back to the kitchen so he could work on the eye-patch.

His mother burst out laughing. He looked back at her. She was leaning against a chair, holding her waist.

"There's nothing funny about that," he said.

She laughed harder. "It wouldn't be funny if it were anybody but you. I mean, you're so odd about costumes and never wanting to be noticed. And here you are dressing T-Bone up like Moshe Dayan!"

"He is a *pirate*, Mom."

"Well, all I saw was the eye-patch." She laughed again, and then tried to stop. She said, "Look, I'm sorry. It's just been such an awful day. I had to type four reports and Mr McBee came in and . . ."

"No, don't apologize. I'm delighted to be the object of such hilarity."

"Now, I'm not laughing at *you*. I'm laughing at . . ." She paused to think of the object of her laughter.

"At what?" T-Bone nudged his knee, and the eye-patch, a flimsy item made of cardboard and black elastic, fluttered into view.

His mother looked away. "Oh, I don't know. I'd better get back to the kitchen." At the door she paused. "May I ask one favour?"

"You can *ask*."

"Let me see T-Bone before you go, when he's all in costume. Just let me see!"

"No, Mom, you'll laugh."

"I won't. I promise."

"You always promise and then you laugh."

"This time I won't."

"It's a terrible thing when a boy cannot believe his own mother."

He glanced back at her. She was in the doorway, watching him with a faint smile on her face. She ran her hands through her short hair.

Once, in the year after his dad left, Simon would have said, "Did you laugh at Dad like this? Isn't that really why he left?" But somehow he had grown beyond that. He liked it when his mother laughed and his dad probably had too.

He looked down at T-Bone and pulled out the pirate hat. He straightened it.

"I want T-Bone to look better than Tony's dog. I want T-Bone to beat him," he admitted.

His mother came back into the room. Her smile was gentler now. "Well, put it on and let me see."

He worked the eye-patch over T-Bone's ears and into place. He opened the hat, set it carefully on his head. He glanced back at his mother.

She was watching with her head cocked to one side. "He'll win," she predicted.

Two for the Show

That afternoon Tony and Miss Vicki and Simon and T-Bone made their way to Harriet Haywood's. Tony was in a mood of great optimism. It was the sight of his aunt's poodle in costume that did it.

Simon was trying to think of this as a period of truce and to take pleasure in the fact that T-Bone was wearing his eye-patch as nicely as if he really had a bad eye. Simon was not going to put the pirate's hat on him until the last moment.

"Miss Vicki could get Best Trick, Simon, if—and I admit this is a big if—if she will stop pulling at her diaper long enough to sit up and bark two times when I say, 'How much are one and one, Miss Vicki?' Have you ever seen her do that?"

"I never saw the dog until five minutes ago, Tony."

"I keep forgetting you don't know my aunt. Well, watch. How much are one and one, Miss Vicki? How much are one and one?"

Miss Vicki was twisted round pulling at her diaper. Tony tugged her leash and she looked up and whined. She couldn't get the diaper off by herself because Tony had made a hole in the diaper for her tail.

"She's not going to do it." Tony leaned down and yanked up the sagging diaper so hard Miss Vicki's back feet left the ground. "Leave your costume alone." He started walking again. "Man, I don't ever want to be a mother."

As they crossed the street, Tony's spirits lifted again. "Maybe there'll be a balloon popping contest. She's good at that. Or a praying contest." He glanced at Simon. "But if she's not in the mood to pray, Simon, she won't pray."

Simon was silent. He reached down and scratched T-Bone behind the ears. T-Bone raised his head and gratefully licked the air.

"There it is," Tony said cheerfully.

They were now approaching Harriet's house. It was a scene of confusion. Cats were mewing sadly in tight-fitting dolls' clothes. A parrot was screaming. A cocker spaniel was trying to get in a position to wet on someone's leg.

Harriet met them at the end of the driveway, her hands on her hips. She looked from Tony to Simon. "You two better not cause any trouble. I mean it."

Tony held up his hands to show he was hiding no bad intentions. "We came to win prizes, Haywood, not to cause trouble."

"That means you too, Simon."

"Would Simon cause trouble?" Tony asked innocently.

"Yes."

Tony made a face behind her back as she turned away. "She's got your number, Pal—Hey, there's Bonfili. What you got, Bonfili?"

Billy Bonfili held up a turtle.

"Bonfili, you brought a turtle?" Tony called in disbelief. "What kind of prize d'you expect to win— Slowest? Man, I thought this was going to be a show for dogs and cats. I didn't know they were going to let reptiles in."

Billy lowered his turtle and moved behind two girls with cats.

"Hey, Bonfili," Tony called, "is that the same turtle you brought to school for Show and Tell in second grade? Remember that, Simon? Teacher, teacher, I'd like to tell about my little friend Snappy."

"Lay off," Simon said.

"You bring a turtle to a pet show, you've got to expect turtle jokes." Tony looked around. "You seen Ackerman?"

"Attention, everybody!" Harriet called from the steps. "We're going to select Best Costume first because some of the dogs are ruining their outfits. First contestant will be Paw-paw Ackerman."

"There she is," Tony said. "She's brought a cat!" He sounded as delighted as if she had brought a unicorn. "Let's get closer."

He pushed his way to the front and stood, eyes glowing, while Cybil displayed Paw-paw in a grass skirt and lei.

66

"Her cat's got them same legs," Tony said to Simon. Then, louder, "Hey, Ackerman, you know what Simon just said. He said your cat's got them same—"

Simon lunged forward and jabbed Tony so hard in the ribs that he choked off the rest.

"What d'you do that for?" Tony demanded. He rubbed his side. "That hurt!"

It was the first time Simon had ever physically attacked anybody. He was stunned at the fury that had sent him, like an out-of-control car, into Tony Angotti. "I slipped," he said.

"Well, watch where you're stepping."

Simon nodded.

Cybil was twisting Paw-paw so that the lower half of his body was doing the hula. Paw-paw's slitted eyes reflected, Simon thought, the same helpless fury he himself felt.

"Second contestant—T-Bone Newton."

Simon managed to get the pirate's hat on T-Bone and lead him forward.

"He should get a prize," Cybil whispered as they passed. "He looks just like Long John Silver."

"Thank you," Simon muttered.

He led T-Bone to the steps and back into place. "I wish I'd thought to bring a little baby bottle," Tony said. "That would clinch it for me." He bent down to straighten Miss Vicki's cap, and it was then that he noticed Miss Vicki had wet her diaper.

He straightened abruptly. "I've got to get out of

here."

"Next contestant—Miss Vicki Angotti!" Harriet called from the steps.

"Miss Vicki's withdrawing," Tony called quickly. He said to Simon, "She's wet her diaper. Let's get out of here."

"Nobody will notice," Simon said loudly. He counted on the sharp eyes of Billy Bonfili to catch the accident. "Go on!" He shoved him forward.

"Hurry *up*," Harriet called. "We've got seventeen contestants in this event."

Billy Bonfili stepped over to see what the trouble was. "Hey, he can't come because his dog wet her diaper," he yelled happily.

Simon sighed, stepping back slightly to avoid being involved in the incident.

"Shut up, Bonfili," Tony said.

"Anybody got an extra diaper?" Billy called. "Tony needs one baaaad. His dog has had a little accident."

"Lay *off*, Bonfili," Tony said.

"It does make the costume authentic," Cybil commented. She grinned and crossed her eyes.

Tony turned from side to side like a bear beset by dogs. Then he yanked Miss Vicki up beneath his arm. "Let's get out of here," he said to Simon.

"I don't want to. T-Bone might win a prize."

"No way. These things are rigged. Harriet's going to give the prizes to her friends. It was stupid of us to come. Let's *go*."

"I'm staying."

Tony glared at him. "Suit yourself," he snapped.

Tony shoved his way through the crowd. He went behind a bush and removed Miss Vicki's diaper and cap. Then he came out pulling her by her leash.

"Hey," Billy called, "you forgot something behind that bush. Why, it's a little, tiny wet dog diaper."

Now that her clothes had been removed, Miss Vicki—perhaps out of gratitude—was trying to say her prayers.

Tony glanced behind him to see what the trouble was with Miss Vicki. "You are *not* praying." He jerked the leash as she again tried to put her head between her paws. "No praying!"

The crowd around Harriet's porch watched in pleased silence as Tony Angotti, head down, walked out of sight, dragging the prayerful Miss Vicki behind him.

That Was Cybil Ackerman

Simon was sitting in his living-room after the pet show. He was slumped on the sofa, staring straight ahead. His emotions were so strong that he was surprised his mother was not questioning him about them. He felt he must reek of pleasure like an onion. He could not wipe the smile off his face.

Simon felt, he decided, a little like that prehistoric fish must have felt, millions of years ago, when he noticed he had tiny legs and decided to try and step out of the water. That first weak step which probably left him jammed in the slime on his belly must have seemed at the time like a useless and stupid thing. Just as his own step today seemed useless and stupid, childish even.

"So much for walking," the fish probably said, writhing back to the sea.

"I will not writhe backwards," Simon said to himself. His smile broadened. He felt better than he had felt in a long time.

Suddenly Cybil Ackerman appeared at the screen door. The sight of her there caused Simon to leap up like a puppet. His feet actually left the floor.

"Good news!" She opened the door, came in and

saw Mrs Newton. "Oh, you must be Simon's mom. Hi!"

Before Simon's mother could nod, Cybil turned back to Simon. "Guess what? Miss Vicki got first prize for Worst Behaved!" She looked delightedly from him to his mother. "It was between her and the cocker spaniel who bit the peekapoo, and we voted. This was after you left."

Simon nodded. After Tony's disgrace, Simon had waited a while and then slipped away too. He hadn't thought anyone noticed. The fact that Cybil had, gave him another pang of pleasure.

"Miss Vicki won by a landslide! It would have been unanimous except for the peekapoo's owner. I'm going over to Tony's house to tell him."

"I'll do that," Simon offered quickly. He was half-way across the living-room, no longer smiling. It came over him in a rush how much he did not want Cybil to go over to Tony Angotti's house. "I was going over there anyway," he lied.

"No, I want to see his face when I tell him."

"But I . . ."

Cybil turned to Mrs Newton. "Did Simon tell you what Miss Vicki did to get Worst Behaved?"

"No."

"Wet her diaper." Cybil grinned. "You'd have to know Tony to appreciate it."

"I appreciate it," Mrs Newton said with a smile.

It came over Simon that he *had* to prevent Cybil from going over to Tony's. He had to keep her *here*.

He made a desperate offer. "You want a Coke?"

"No, I've got to go." She swirled. "Say good-bye to everybody, Paw-paw." She made Paw-paw wave to each of them.

Mrs Newton waved back. It was the first time Simon had seen his mother wave to a cat, but that, he thought, was the effect Cybil had on people. Swinging Paw-paw under her arm, she went out of the door.

Simon stood in the middle of the rug as Cybil's footsteps faded into the distance. His thoughts went with her as she crossed Brock Street, turned down Oak, went up the Angottis' driveway. As he thought of her ringing the bell, his face twisted with misery.

"Who was that girl?" Simon's mother asked.

Simon looked at her. It sounded like the end of "The Lone Ranger" shows when somebody asks in an important voice, "Who was that masked man?" and somebody answers in an equally important voice, "That was the Lone Ranger."

Simon answered in an equally important voice, "That was Cybil Ackerman."

He did not move. He was overcome by how quickly tides could turn in love and war, how quickly up could become down, victory, defeat.

"That was Cybil Ackerman," he repeated to himself.

And it was not like there were dozens of Cybil Ackermans, he realized. There was only one. And in the world that swirled in confusion and conflict around him, she was an oasis, a patch of fresh air, a circle of peace.

He started for his room, stumbled over the rug and missed a step. "Are you all right?" his mother asked quickly.

"I'm fine," he said with careful cheer.

"Your face looks flushed."

"I'm hot."

"Simon . . ."

"Let me alone."

He closed the door behind him.

The Saddest Sentence

When Simon was in third grade the teacher Mr Romano asked the class to write in twenty words or less the saddest sentence they could think of.

Billy Bonfili's sentence was: Last summer I almost drowned in front of my cousins and they laughed.

Cybil's was: My cat Paw-paw has been missing for three weeks and I think he's dead.

Simon's was: Last summer my mom sent me to Camp Okiechobie to make up for the fact that my dad left and on the third day I got the worst case of poison ivy the counsellors had ever seen and finally it reached my eyes and I had to be led blindly to the toilets by a boy named Mervin Rollins who refused to tell me if there were any Daddy-long-legs on the toilet seat.

Simon's sentence was way too long, of course, but Mr Romano gave him an A anyway because he admitted it was hard to condense that much sadness into twenty words.

After that, Simon had often tried to create the saddest sentence in the world. He knew he had it with "My father has gone," but he still kept writing. So far he had written twenty-seven.

Now he tried for twenty-eight.

"I was a jar of peanut butter in the class play and I stepped out and said my line perfectly (Peanut butter is a nutritious food and good in sandwiches or on crackers), but when I stepped back into place, I bumped into Billy Bonfili who shoved me back so hard that I pushed Harriet Haywood who was unsteady in an ill-fitting cottage cheese carton and who sat down on the stage and couldn't get up until me and the green beans helped her and Cybil looked at me and did not grin and cross her eyes and later the green beans told the teacher I had done it on purpose and the whole thing made me wish I had never seen, heard of or tasted peanut butter."

Way too long, Simon decided, too tiresome, too many who's, and anyway nobody cares about the feelings of a jar of peanut butter.

He was sitting at his desk as he wrote the sentence, waiting for the bell to ring. The sign "Peanut Butter" which he had worn in the play was on the floor under his feet. The dusty prints of his tennis shoes had blurred the letters.

Simon reread his sentence and then folded it to take home. One day he would have a collection of sad sentences worthy of being donated to a library. They would have a special room—The Simon Newton Collection—and people would pass through and marvel at the sadness of the sentences in the glass cases.

The bell rang, startling him out of his thoughts. He

got up, sighing, and picked up his books.

The sacks of potatoes jostled him as he went into the hall. He barely felt the jabs of their elbows.

He had the eerie, crystal-ball feeling that there would be another, newer, sadder sentence in the very near future. It was such a strong feeling that he could almost hear the sympathetic sighs of the viewers as they looked into the last case and read—

It was just as well, he thought, that he didn't know what.

The Newer Sadder Sentence

In the week that followed, Simon sometimes felt he was a yo-yo he went up and down so quickly. In school he could not concentrate because he had to keep watching Tony Angotti who was watching Cybil and then watching Cybil to see if she was watching Tony. His neck began to ache with all this unnatural straining.

"Eyes front," Miss McFawn said again and again.

Sometimes to Simon's surprise she would add, "Tony," and Simon would know Tony had been looking at Cybil and he hadn't caught him. Then he would glance back quickly himself. Cybil would be writing or looking for something in her notebook, and Simon would feel instantly better.

One day after school when Simon and Tony were walking home, Tony said, "Everybody likes me but Cybil Ackerman," in a depressed way.

Tony's genuine dismay made Simon feel wonderful. His steps quickened with pleasure. But then he began to analyse that statement and he slowed down. Everybody did *not* like Tony. He himself could name at least ten people who didn't like Tony, starting with Simon's mother, Miss Ellis, Mr Repokis, Annette,

Harriet Haywood, Billy Bonfili ... And if Tony could be wrong about that, then he could also be wrong about Cybil not liking him.

"What makes you say that?" Simon asked carefully.

"Oh, I don't know. Do you think she likes me?"

"I don't know. She's the kind of person who likes everybody." He paused then added, "No matter what they're like."

"Yeah, there's no reason why she *wouldn't* like me." He held up his hands as if he were testing for rain. "She probably does like me. Thanks, Pal." And he walked on, obviously feeling much better.

Behind him, Simon followed, feeling much worse. "What do *I* know," he said, but his target was out of range.

But even with all these ups and downs, he was not prepared for Thursday.

Thursday had been an ordinary school day, one of those days so boring that when his mother would ask him to tell her one thing that had happened, he would not be able to. He would have to make up something that had happened another day to satisfy her.

Not once had he caught Tony looking at Cybil or Cybil looking anywhere but at her papers or through her notebook, and he had been lulled into a feeling of warm security.

I was walking home, with Simon whistling happily under his breath, when the blow fell. Tony Angotti said, "Cybil Ackerman *does* like me."

78

Simon stumbled over a root. He looked up to see a smirk on Tony's face. "What?" He felt his cheeks begin to burn.

"Cybil Ackerman *does* like me."

"Yesterday you said she didn't."

"That was yesterday." Another smirk.

"But what happened? I didn't see her even look at you. What makes you think she likes you?"

"She must. She's going to the movies with me."

"What?" Simon stumbled again. "What? You asked Cybil to go to the movies with you?"

Tony nodded.

Simon kept staring at Tony. He could not believe it. He had known that some time in the future, all of them would be taking girls to movies and maybe even to dances, but that was years in the future. It was as unthinkable now as their joining the army.

A runner passed them. Simon heard the man's rasping breath, felt a spray of sweat, heard the slap of shoes against the pavement.

Sometimes it seemed to Simon that the whole world was running, that someone had yelled, "Fire," and everybody had started running, with his father leading the pack. And he, like the prehistoric fish, couldn't take a step without plopping belly-down in the mire.

"There's just one catch," Tony said.

"What?"

"She won't go unless you and Haywood come too."

Simon stopped as abruptly as if he had run into a brick wall. "What?"

"You and Haywood have to come to the movies with us." Tony spoke as slowly and carefully as if he was speaking to someone with concussion.

"Wait a minute. Do you mean *I* would have a date with Harriet Haywood?" Simon's voice was higher than he had ever heard it.

"Well, it's not actually a date," Tony explained. "We aren't going to pay their way. I was very careful about that." He touched his forehead. "I told them we would meet them *inside*, *beyond* the candy counter. How's that for planning? We won't even have to buy them popcorn!"

"I'm not going to the movies with Harriet Haywood," Simon said flatly.

"You have to."

"I don't."

"But I've already set it up. I've told Harriet you wanted to make up for overturning her in the play. You made a fool of her, Simon. I should think you'd want to . . ."

He kept shaking his head.

Tony sighed with disappointment. "Then I'll have to get Bonfili."

"What?" Simon looked up. Tony's face, honest and open, looked back at him with regret.

"Harriet said she would go with either you or Bonfili and so since you won't go . . ." He shrugged.

Simon moaned beneath his breath. He put one

hand to his forehead. It was one of those moments in a war, he decided, when the first inkling of failure comes, when that first sickening awareness that the war can be lost, that *you* can be defeated, comes and stays and grows. Grown men must tremble, he thought, deep inside them like volcanoes. He himself felt sick.

"I'll go," he muttered.

Tony clapped him on the back, almost sending him to his knees on the sidewalk. "I'll tell them it's all set."

"Yes, tell them that."

Tony hurried off, leaving Simon alone. Simon kept standing there. All week he had been trying to prevent Cybil from looking at Tony – just from looking at him, and while he was congratulating himself on his success, he learned that somehow, without those looks, they had arranged a *date*. It was like the enemy taking the castle without the moat.

He turned around on the sidewalk like a person starting a game of Blind Man's Bluff.

Slowly he began to make his way home. He walked like an old man trying to get used to new glasses. He tripped over kerbs, tree roots, blades of grass.

It was, he decided, like Camp Okiechobie again, being led blindly to the toilets by Mervin Rollins. He could almost hear Mervin calling in his clear, young voice, "There are no Daddy-long-legs on the toilet seat."

And when he got home at last and sank down on

the front steps, he even thought he heard, once again, the silken sigh of crushed Daddy-long-legs.

The fact that he had now, without even trying, written an absolutely perfect sad sentence—I have a date with Harriet Haywood—was no comfort at all.

An Hour of Misfortune

Simon stood by his bed looking out the window. It was dark, but he had not turned on the light.

On this, the evening before his date with Harriet Haywood, darkness seemed appropriate. All day, as he had sat in school with his head down—never looking up once to see if Tony was looking at Cybil or Cybil looking at Tony or—worse, if Harriet Haywood was looking at *him*, he had wished for darkness.

Now that the miracle had happened, he could not enjoy it. There had been a letter from his father that afternoon. He was in Arizona in a deserted mining town. He and some friends were working the mine, digging out turquoise. When they earned enough money, his father said, they were going to build a raft and sail to South America.

"He's obsessed," his mother said when she finished the letter. She let it drop to the table as if it were heavy. "He's digging for turquoise when every single person in the world has as much turquoise as they can possibly wear." She shook her head. "And what will he do in South America? Can you tell me that?"

He shook his head. The letters upset them both, only they reacted differently. His mother asked question after question, one after another, questions that had no answers. Even a week later she would interrupt his studying to say, "And why on earth would he . . ." Simon had asked the questions at first too, only now he had stopped.

The image he had of his father was getting blurred, altered by all the pictures he'd seen of hermits and wild men, miners now, and men who let the ocean sweep them away on rafts. He could not remember his father's face at all.

Once he had believed he would be like his father when he grew up. It was more than a matter of genes. He wanted to be like him.

He would wear old woollen jackets and patched jeans and let his hair grow and protest against nuclear power. He would no longer fear wasps and poison ivy and would genuinely care about the natural habitat of the snail fish. He would eat mostly beans and rice.

But this afternoon, sitting at the table, looking at the letter that lay between him and his mother, he no longer believed it.

It wasn't just that he could not imagine himself digging for turquoise in a mine hundreds of feet below ground or living in a forest. It was that he was still trying to go forward somehow, fighting through the confusion and complications, against all biological odds, and his father had gone so far backward that he wanted to go to South America on a raft.

He sighed, watched the street below where a dog was checking out the garbage cans. The dog found a piece of meat paper and went away.

And in his date with Harriet Haywood, Simon thought, the first terrible social obligation of his life, an event so complicated and awful it made him feel sick, in this was the final proof of his difference. It had never once occurred to him to run.

It was odd. The original reason for accepting the date was so that he could be there to keep an eye on Cybil and Tony. But this was no longer true. He didn't want to see what they did. And yet here he was, going on the date as bravely as Daniel went into the lion's den.

But then maybe his father had done this too, he thought, gone on dates he didn't want to go on, done things he didn't want to do, until one day . . .

He turned abruptly and walked into the living-room. T-Bone was lying on the hearth.

Simon lay down beside the dog with his cheek against the cool slate. "T-Bone, I've got some unfortunate news. I have a date with Harriet Haywood."

He was pleased that his voice was calm, normal, nothing in his tone to alarm the dog.

T-Bone opened his eyes but did not lift his head. He thumped his tail once on the hearth.

"She's as big as a woman, T-Bone."

Thump.

"A grown woman." He paused. "Make that an

85

*over*grown woman."

As he said that, a picture of Harriet Haywood came into his mind, bigger even than life and with the kind of stern authority of an adult. He remembered her, hands on her hips, saying, "You'd better not cause any trouble," at the pet show. It was like having a date with Miss McFawn, he decided, and shuddered.

At almost the same moment he thought of Cybil. He remembered her running out of her house once with Clara's diary. It was during second grade, the peak—he thought then—of his love.

And Clara had come after her and Cybil had scooted up in the mimosa and, legs dangling in the sunlight, pretended to read from the diary.

"Mom! Cybil's got my diary."

"Cybil!"

"Mom, you ought to read this yourself, especially Saturday, September ninth!"

"Cybilllll!"

"Oh, here's your old diary," Cybil said, dropping it. "Anyway, if it makes you feel any better, I can't read cursive writing yet."

Then she had seen Simon standing at the edge of the street. "Simon, come on up!"

He had climbed up, feeling better and stronger with each climb as if the air itself was getting cleaner, rarer, less polluted. When he got there at last she said, "I don't like Miss Ellis, do you?"

"No."

"You know what my sister calls her?"

"No."

"Devilled Egg."

That alone—the perfect assessment of Miss Ellis—would have made the climb worthwhile.

"Your sisters," he said, paying them his highest compliment, "remind me of you."

"Yes, we all look alike, and d'you know what? My mom is beautiful. Have you ever seen her?" He shook his head. "Well, she's *beautiful*, only she has very weak genes. We've got my father's eyes, my father's skin, my father's hair, my father's legs, everything. Guess what we've got from my mother?" He shook his head again. "Skimpy ear lobes. Look!" She lifted her hair. "None of us can ever wear ear-rings."

He had been so charmed that he almost fell out of the tree like a drunken bird.

Simon glanced over at T-Bone who was asleep again. He said, "I had a nightmare about my date with Harriet, T-Bone. I was on a TV show called 'Take Your Pick' and I had to decide whether I would go on a date with Harriet or with a gorilla and I couldn't decide and the clock was ticking and they were in glass booths—Harriet and the gorilla—and I was running back and forth, from one booth to the other, and by accident the gorilla's door opened and Harriet thought I'd picked the gorilla and she came out and hit me over the head with an umbrella.

"Well, my mom came in then and woke me up and said, 'Simon, you were having a nightmare.' And I

87

said, 'Yes.' Then I said, 'Oh, by the way, I have a date this Saturday,' in a normal voice as if I had been dating all my life. She said, 'Oh, with that nice little girl who was over here last week—Cybil Somebody.' And I said, 'No, with the tub of blubber.' End of conversation between me and my mom."

Suddenly Simon put his arm around T-Bone and buried his face in the fur of T-Bone's neck. He hadn't done this in a long time, but the dog smelled exactly the same, felt exactly the same. He himself felt compelled to act as he used to.

"Oh, T-Bone, I don't want to go," he said, feeling the childish words coming in a comfortable rush. "I don't want to go on a date with Harriet Haywood. I don't want to have dates. T-Bone, help me, bite me, do something, anything. Give me a dog disease. T-Bone, do something!"

Lick.

Simon sat up and looked at the dog. "T-Bone, I must say that you have been a real help and consolation in my hour of misfortune. Thank you."

Thump.

A Date with
Harriet Haywood

The day of Simon's date was beautiful and mild, and Simon made his way to the Mall under a cloudless sky.

He began walking slower when he got to the Mall parking lot. His determination, which he now estimated to have the size and permanence of an ice cube, began to grow even smaller as he crossed the warm pavement. He stopped beside a van.

This would be, he thought suddenly, the absolutely perfect moment for his father to kidnap him. His father could leap from the van, beard flying, snatch him up, toss him inside and roar off to ancient forests and turquoise mines, or wherever real day-to-day living didn't exist. Only Harriet Haywood, cheated out of her date, would mind. Hands on hips, eyes narrowed, she would say, "I *knew* he wouldn't behave!" He shuddered slightly as he left the shelter of the van.

Suddenly Tony Angotti burst through the Mall doors. He ran across the parking lot, dodging cars like he was on the football field.

"Disaster," he gasped when he got to Simon. The force of his movement caused them to swing round like children on the playground.

"What happened?" Simon asked. His voice rose with sudden hope. "Harriet didn't come?"

"Worse! They're waiting *outside* the movie theatre." He grabbed Simon's shoulders and shook him to get the meaning to go down. "I told them *inside*, you know so we have to *pay!*"

"Well—"

"And now they're *outside!*" His eyes shifted to Simon's pocket. "How much money have you got?"

"Three dollars."

"Well, it's two dollars to get in, and that's what I've got—two dollars! And even for that I have to stoop down and pretend I'm a child!"

"That won't work for Harriet. She's big, Tony. I was thinking about that last night. She's—"

"Shut up and think!"

"Maybe we should just go home," Simon said while Tony wrung his hands. "Forget it."

"We are not going to forget it," Tony said firmly. He began pulling Simon towards the Mall by the front of his shirt.

"Well, if we haven't got the money—"

"We'll tell them to go on inside," Tony said with sudden inspiration. "How does this sound? We'll tell them you have to buy something in Penney's for your mother. We'll tell them to save us some seats. All right now, let's go in and try it."

Cybil and Harriet were waiting—Tony was right—outside the theatre. They were both wearing skirts and blouses. This alarmed Simon. He thought the only time girls wore skirts and blouses was to church and special occasions. He did not want anyone to think of this as a special occasion. He began to walk slower.

"Now back me up," Tony said. He approached the girls and stood by Cybil. "Look, Simon's got a little problem. Me and him have got to go into Penney's for a minute and get something for his mom. You go on inside and we'll be right with you."

"We'll wait for you out here," Harriet said firmly. She looked so big in her skirt and blouse that she seemed to block the whole front of the theatre.

"Inside, *inside*." Tony pushed them towards the ticket seller. "You'll have to save the seats."

"But we're the first people here," Harriet said. She turned and faced them. Her hands were on her hips. "The whole theatre is empty."

"Yeah, but me and Simon like to sit in the front row, don't we, Pal?"

This time Tony spun Harriet round with such force and skill that she found herself directly in front of the ticket booth. "How many?" the woman asked in a bored voice.

"One—child," Harriet said through tight lips. She glanced back with fury at Tony and Simon as she bent her knees.

"One," said Cybil.

Tony pulled Simon towards Penney's. "Don't look back," he said. "It might be a trick." He shook his head. "If they don't buy those tickets, well, we'll just have to keep on going."

They went into Penney's and hid in the shoe department. Tony peered around the display of high heels. "They've either gone in or they've gone home," he reported.

"They've gone in," Simon said pessimistically.

"Let's go then."

They walked back to the theatre and Tony said, "Did two girls buy tickets and go inside a minute ago?"

"Were they wearing skirts and blouses?" the woman in the booth asked.

"I didn't notice what they were wearing," Tony said. "One's redheaded and one's fat."

"They were wearing skirts and blouses," Simon said quickly.

"Then, yeah, they're inside."

"Did they buy popcorn and candy?"

"No."

"Bad news," Tony said as he bent his knees. "One—child."

Simon bought popcorn and they made their way into the theatre. They did not have any trouble spotting Harriet and Cybil because they were the only two people there. They were sitting in the front row, talking to each other over two empty seats.

Harriet looked back and said, "Here they come and look! They didn't buy anything at Penney's. I told you they just didn't want to pay our way."

"Penney's was all out of unmentionables in his mom's size," Tony explained quickly, slipping into the seat beside Cybil.

Simon sat by Harriet. "Popcorn?" he asked.

"Thanks."

She took the box and began to eat. Simon watched as the top pieces, yellow with butter, disappeared into her mouth, then the dry middle pieces. When she got to the bottom where the crumbs were, she offered the box back to Simon.

He shook his head.

"You're sure you don't want any?"

He nodded.

"Well, if you're sure." She turned up the container and drank the crumbs. Then she said, "I'm thirsty, aren't you?"

Simon got up dutifully. He made his way to the back of the theatre and bought a small Coke with the rest of his money.

"Thanks," Harriet said. "Did they have any Jujubes? Now I've got my braces off I can eat anything."

"They didn't have any."

"How about Milk Duds?"

"No."

The lights went down at last and Simon sat staring up at the screen like a sick dog.

"You want some Coke?" Harriet asked.

He shook his head.

She polished it off and began to chew on the ice.

Simon's eyes misted over, either from the nearness of the screen or the fact that his whole adult life was stretching ahead of him as a series of dates, one Harriet Haywood after another.

Tony nudged him. Simon looked over in time to see Tony reaching for Cybil Ackerman's hand. He turned his eyes quickly to the screen and watched the images waver in the mist.

"The scary part's coming up," Harriet told him. "My sister's already seen this. She says to keep your eyes on the door because that's where the monster's hiding. She says the door bursts open just when they reach the cages and the monster comes through. She says it'll really scare you if you're not expecting it."

"I'll be expecting it," Simon said.

"Oh, listen, don't let me ruin the fun for you!" She nudged him with her elbow.

The chances of ruining something that was non-existent seemed slight.

"You won't," he promised, shifting to the far side of his seat where he would, he hoped, be out of range.

His Own Worst Enemy

Harriet walked Simon home. This, he felt, was the equivalent of being marched home by the principal. He only spoke two words. Twice Harriet asked him what he was thinking about, and twice he answered, "Nothing."

When they got to his house Harriet said, "You know, I think Cybil's feelings were hurt."

"What?" He had already started to turn into his driveway, but now he paused. This was the first interest he had shown in anything, so Harriet looked pleased.

"You know, because you wanted to be with me."

"What?"

"Oh, you know." She gave Simon a playful poke, and he put his hand over the spot to protect it. "Cybil thought she was going to be with you at the movies and then this morning Tony called me and said that you wanted to be with me, that you would not come unless you could sit by me, and for me to tell Cybil when we . . ."

"*What?*"

"Well, Cybil had agreed to go to the movies with you because she didn't like Tony. It was all set—you and Cybil, me and Tony. I don't like Tony either, but I wanted to see the movie. Only then, Tony said you wanted to be with me and . . ."

She continued, but Simon no longer heard her. This was like something out of a soap opera—lies and plots and misunderstandings. Rage began to burn in his chest like a hot coal.

"Good-bye," he told Harriet.

"Wait. I'm not through."

"Good-bye."

He went into the house, walked through to the kitchen and waited for his mother to ask what was wrong. His face had to be so flushed she would go straight for the thermometer. She glanced up and then back down at a cake she was icing.

"How does that look?" she asked, turning the plate around on the table.

"Fine," he snapped.

"I'm going to a supper tonight—it's Parents Without Partners—and I want my cake to look, you know—edible." She smiled.

He waited, then said, "Is this Parents Without Partners like a *date?*" He wanted to remind her that he had just come from such an event himself. For the first time in his life he actually wanted to talk.

"No, it's just people getting together."

"Oh." He waited again, and then said in a rush, "Aren't you going to ask me how my date was?"

"Yes, how was it?"

"Terrible, awful, horrible, miserable, sickening

and infuriating."

She made a face. "I'm glad you had such a good time."

"Thanks."

"What went wrong?"

"Everything. I was supposed to be with Cybil and Tony tricked me into being with Harriet. Mom, she poked me all during the movie. I *hate* Tony!"

"Don't be too hard on him."

"Mom! When I used to like Tony you were always putting him down and wanting me to get new friends, and now that I hate him, you're defending him!"

"No, what worried me when you and Tony were friends, was that he took advantage of you and you seemed to always get the short end of the stick and take the blame—and you never seemed to know what he was doing. Now that you see Tony for what he is, well, I feel better about your being friends."

"We *aren't* friends."

"Tony is his own worst enemy."

"No, he's got me now."

She looked at him. "Do you remember when you were in first grade and Tony moved here and he sat behind you and that whole year he claimed he had got an unlucky desk?"

"I don't remember that."

"Every time he got a bad grade, he would start hitting his desk—you told me this, and you told me that one time you went home with him and he had his report card and it was bad and his mother thumped him on the head with her ring and he burst out crying and said. 'What d'you expect? I told you I'd got the unlucky desk.'"

"I remember his mom hitting him."

"Well, anyway, that, to me, is Tony. Tony is probably going to go through his whole life without knowing what he's like or why things happen to him or why things don't happen to him or what other people think or feel. It's sad." She looked at him, waiting.

"I still hate him," he said.

She smiled. "Okay, hate him." She glanced down at her cake and picked it up. "Now, I am proud of that cake," she said. "I've got out of the habit of cooking and I bet I haven't made a cake in—" She paused, remembering the exact day she had lost interest in cooking.

"In two and a half years," Simon said.

"Two and a half years."

Simon got off the stool and walked into the living-room. "I hope you didn't fill up on popcorn and candy," his mother called after him.

"That is not possible on a date with Harriet Haywood," he called back.

"Because your supper's ready."

"Good, I've got to go somewhere tonight."

"Not over to Tony's. Not till you cool down."

"No, not over to Tony's."

The Victory

Simon stood at the edge of Cybil's yard, waiting respectfully with his hands behind his back. Cybil's sister, Clarice, was having a Miss America pageant on the front lawn. It was the talent portion of the production, and Clarice was dancing to "God Bless America" which someone was playing on the piano inside.

Simon had come there right after supper. He had decided that this time he would not pretend to be looking for something. There had been enough lies and pretences. He would walk straight up to the door like an adult, ring the bell and ask to speak to Cybil. He would then try to explain the confusion of the afternoon by uttering the understatement of the year. "I did not really want to be with Harriet Haywood at the movies."

His intention had been stalled by the Miss America pageant, but as soon as it was over he would proceed to the front door.

Clarice finished her dance. She said loudly, "I want to be Miss America so that I can bring peace to all the world through my dancing."

Applause. Clarice went back and stood proudly on the front steps with the other three candidates. Simon shifted restlessly. He wondered if he could slip past the candidates without disturbing the whole production.

Too late. A baton-twirling routine to "God Bless America" began. Simon continued to stand respectfully on the sidelines.

He looked up at the house, listened to the music. The Ackerman house was like a commercial for living, he thought, an advertisement to show how zestful ordinary, day-to-day life can be.

As he stood there he began to realize that it was Cybil at the piano. He could not see in the window, of course, and never intended to try to do so again, but somehow he was sure it was Cybil, willingly, energetically playing "God Bless America" again and again. A warm feeling came over him.

The baton routine ended. Now the decision of judges—Clarice is the new Miss America! Simon broke his respectful stance long enough to applaud.

"Why do *you* get to be Miss America?" the baton twirler snapped. Her hands were on her hips. Simon thought this was the way the losers would really act if the TV cameras weren't there.

"Because the judges picked me," Clarice said coolly.

"The judges are your sisters!"

"I can't help that!"

"Well, I better get to be Miss Congeniality or I'm going home!"

Simon slipped past them, up the steps, and to the

front door. He rang the bell.

It was Cybil who came to the door. "Oh, hi," she said.

His plan, which had seemed so sensible, so adult on the way over, now seemed stupid. Finally he managed to get out his statement. "I just wanted to tell you that I didn't really want to be with Harriet this afternoon."

"Oh, I know that."

"You do?"

"Tony told me. He got mad and said I didn't know how lucky I was to sit by him. He said most girls would consider it an honour. And you know who he thinks he looks like?"

"Donny Osmond."

"Yes! And you know what he did? He tried to hold my hand in the movies. And you know what I did? I pinched his hand right in the palm where it really hurts. Didn't you hear him gasp?"

"I was watching the movie."

Clarice stormed by. "Just because *I* got to be Miss America everybody's gone home!" She turned back to Cybil. "And you were supposed to play 'There She Is, Miss America' so I could come down the steps and—everything is *ruined*. Mom, Cybil ruined my Miss America Pageant!"

"Cybil," Mrs Ackerman called tiredly from the living-room.

Cybil grinned and crossed her eyes. "You want to go bike riding?" she asked suddenly.

Simon felt a stab of despair. "I don't have a bike."

"You can borrow Clara's. Clara! Can Simon borrow your bike?"

"If he's careful and puts some air in the front tyre," Clara called back.

"We'll stop at the gas station," Cybil told Simon as she led him to the garage.

As they started out of the driveway Simon glanced at Cybil and paused. Her red hair was streaming behind her in the wind. It made Simon think of flags and banners and bands. She looked back, "Are you coming?"

"Yes!"

He had a brief struggle with his pedals and his knee hit the straw basket which was tied on the handlebars. Then his feet and legs got straightened out, and he pedalled after Cybil.

They rode down the hill in silence. As they turned the corner in a wide arc, Simon suddenly thought that his father was missing a lot out there in that turquoise mine. It was the first time he had felt sorry for his father rather than for himself. Because in this world, with all its troubles, even if you had to sit by Harriet Haywood in the movies in the afternoon, you could still be riding beside Cybil Ackerman in the evening.

He thought again about that prehistoric creature who finally got up on his legs in the slime, stepped forward and found himself not bellied down but— miracle!—on a bicycle, cool wind in his face, going thirty miles an hour with Cybil Ackerman at his side. Millions of years of evolution bypassed in a moment. It seemed so clear a transformation that the whole process flashed through his mind, with himself the final glorious frame.

"We better stop at the gas station," Cybil said over her shoulder. "Clara's real particular about her things. Let's cut through here."

It was Oak Street—Tony's street. Simon felt his heart beat faster. "All right," he said quickly. He steered to the right beside her.

He glanced up as they approached Tony's house. He braked slightly when he saw that Tony was sitting on the front steps with Pap-pap. He wanted to give them time to see him. Pap-pap was getting ready to cry about something. He already had his handkerchief out, twisting it into a rope. But Tony was staring at the street.

When Tony saw the bicycles, and who was riding them, he got quickly to his feet. His mouth was hanging open in surprise.

Risking an accident, Simon lifted one hand in a half wave. Then he clutched the handlebars again. The thought of wrecking Clara's bicycle made him decide not to even glance at Tony again.

"Wait a minute," he heard Tony yell. "Hey, come back. Wait a minute. I'll come with you guys. Hey, wait! I'll get Annette's bike!"

Simon pedalled faster again, and he and Cybil rode down the hill, around the corner, and down Elm

Street. Simon's smile was so broad that his teeth were getting dry. He felt he had had his victory. That wave—just a lift of the hand without wrecking the bike—that was all he needed to acknowledge it.

He felt he had seen something like this in an old news-reel. It was so clear he had to have seen it. A victorious general came riding through a war-torn city, and he graciously—just like Simon—lifted one hand to the crowd. The crowd waved flags, shouted, wept. There was none of that celebrating for Simon's appearance, and yet the result was the same, he thought. The war was over.

Simon glanced at Cybil. He wondered if she would like to ride past Harriet Haywood's and lift *her* hand. No, he decided, she was bigger than that. He watched as she made a left hand signal to turn into the gas station. He did the same.

"Do you know how to use this?" Cybil asked as they stopped in front of the air hose.

"No," he admitted.

"I'll show you."

Her red head bent over the tyre. Her curls blew in the wind. She glanced up at Simon.

Abruptly he abandoned his pose as the triumphant general. After all, the war was over. This was the real world, and he better learn how it worked.

He knelt beside her and watched.